GRUMP GROAN GROWL

By bell hooks
Illustrated by Chris Raschka

Hyperion Books for Children

New York

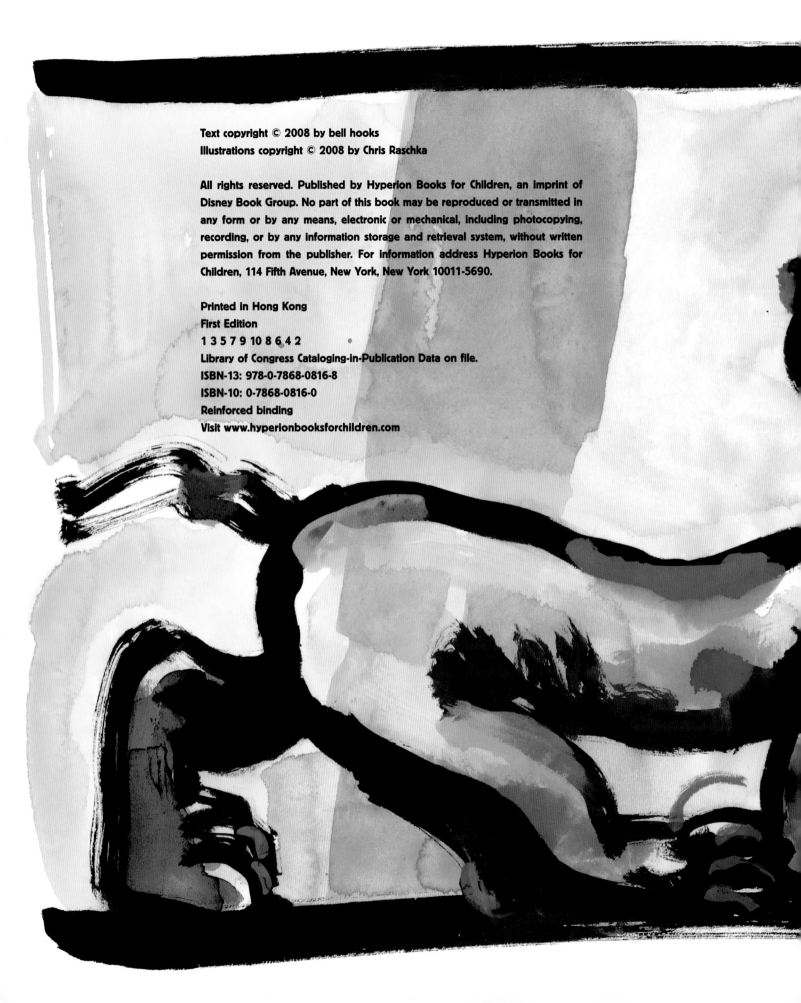

Printed in Hong Kong
First Edition
1 3 5 7 9 10 8 6 4 2
Library of Congress Cataloging-in-Publication Data on file.
ISBN-13: 978-0-7868-0816-8
ISBN-10: 0-7868-0816-0
Reinforced binding
Visit www.hyperionbooksforchildren.com

for MARCUS
best boy—
beloved reader
—bh

For bell
—CR

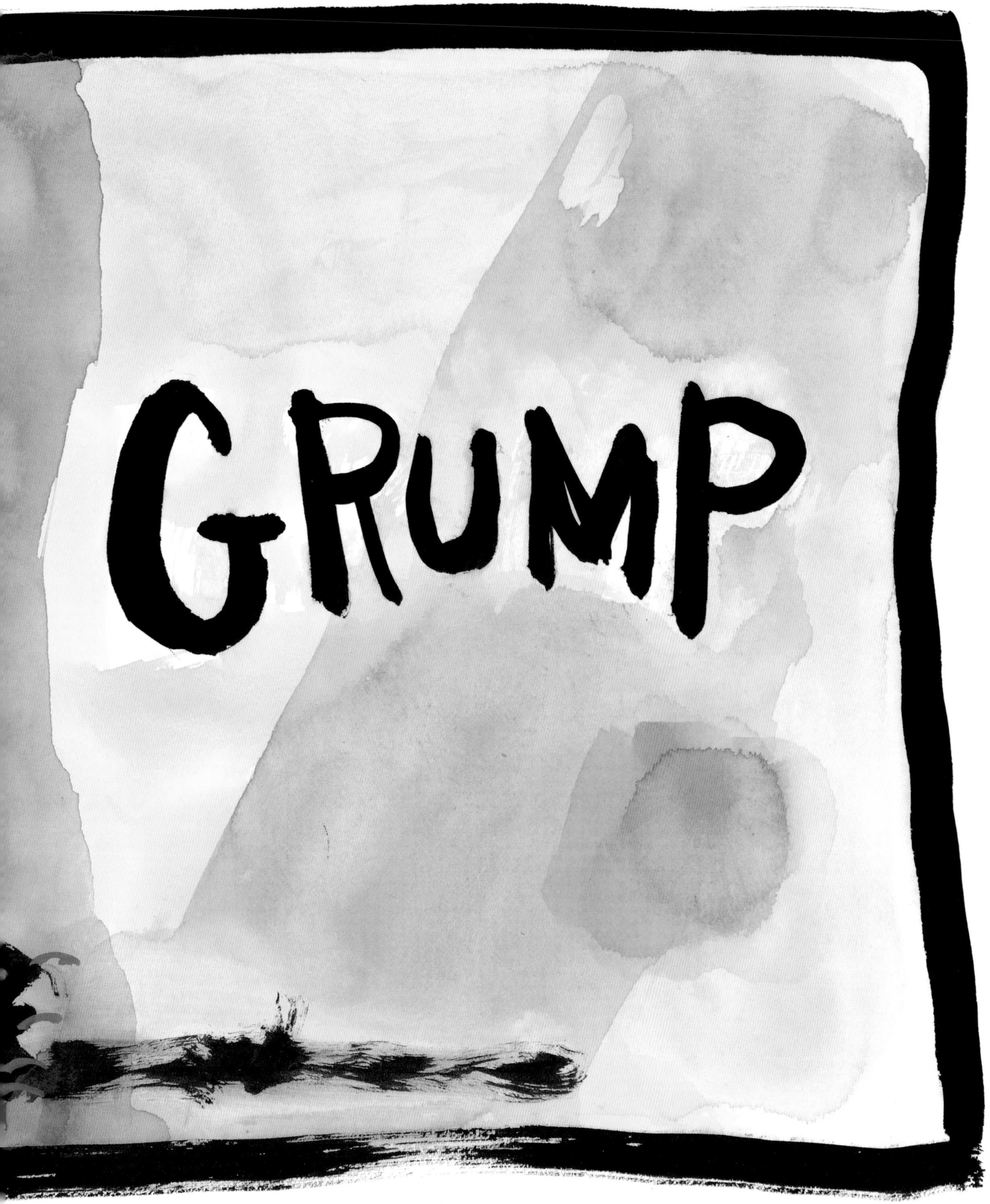
GRUMP

GROAN

GROWL

MooD

on the prowl

CAN'T STAND OUTSIDE

ALL I AM IS

BAD MOOD
on the PROWL

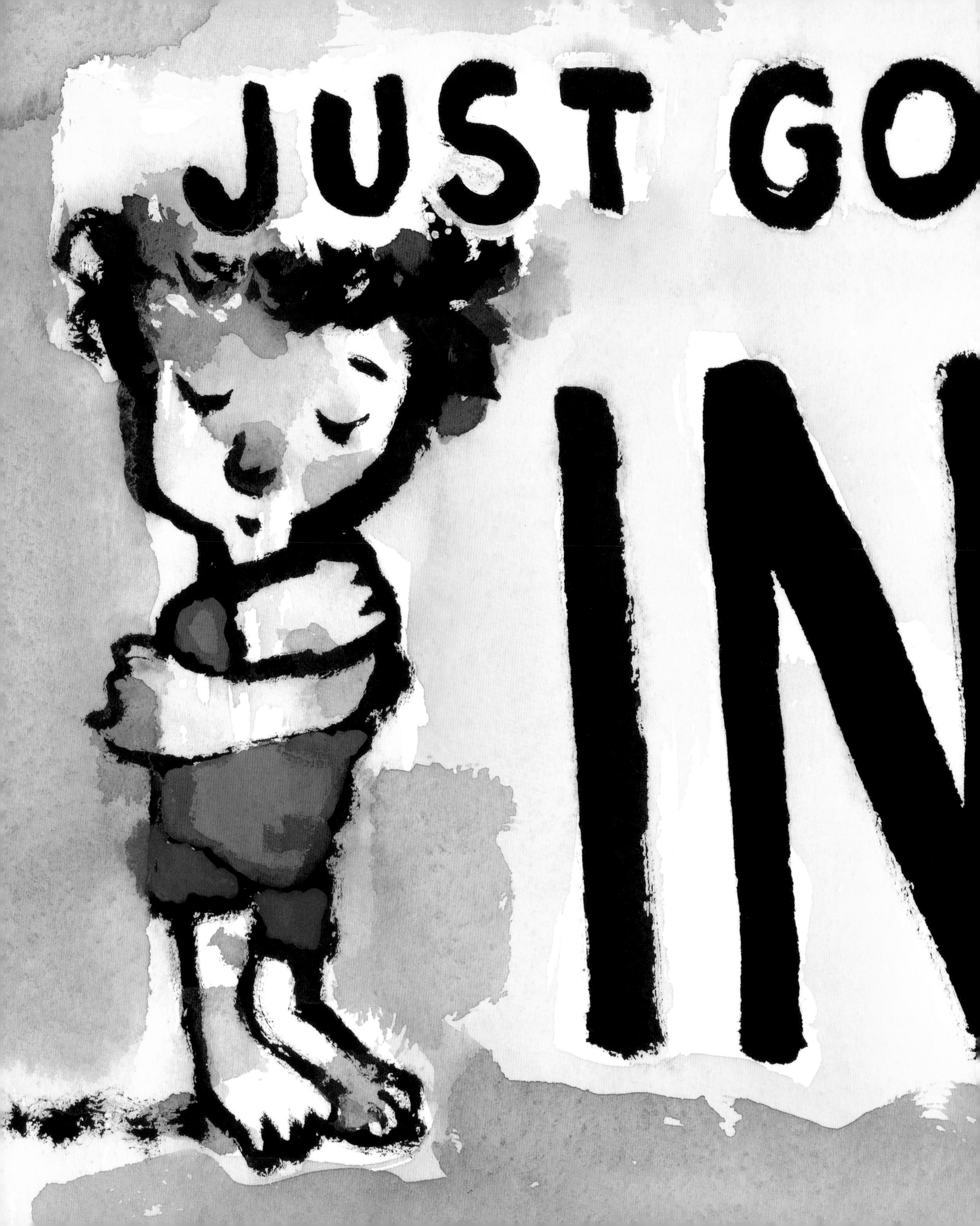
JUST GO
IN

Just let those
feelings
BE